EX-MONK

JAMES G. PORTO

America Star Books

© 2014 by James G. Porto.
All rights reserved. No part of this book may be reproduced, stored in a retrieval system or transmitted in any form or by any means without the prior written permission of the publishers, except by a reviewer who may quote brief passages in a review to be printed in a newspaper, magazine or journal.

First printing

All characters in this book are fictitious, and any resemblance to real persons, living or dead, is coincidental.

America Star Books has allowed this work to remain exactly as the author intended, verbatim, without editorial input.

Softcover 9781632494405
PUBLISHED BY AMERICA STAR BOOKS, LLLP
www.americastarbooks.com

Printed in the United States of America
Seneca Falls Library
47 Cayuga Street
Seneca Falls, N.Y. 13148

I wish to dedicate this book to:

My beloved Professor, Dr. Tyson Anderson, PhD, who once told me that he realized when he was laughing, he was actually crying. At first, I thought he was describing his reaction to reading the papers I submitted.

Ms. Kathryn Taylor, who should have a book dedicated to her. She woke me up.

John Maag-Tanchak (who could write a better book than I) and Karin Maag-Tanchack (who could translate the book into German).

Paul Walters, who knew me before I ever did.

Charley and Edward Morse, my first friends.

Steve Mitchell, my brother from another mother.

Ms. Brenda Jean Riley Bowman, a walking blessing.

My sisters, Mary and Eileen, their children, my nieces, nephews and grand-niece, all children and those with the heart of a child.

PROLOGUE

GENESIS

Sleepy Hollow is located on the eastern bank of the Hudson River, about thirty miles north of midtown Manhattan in New York City. Washington Irving is buried in Sleepy Hollow Cemetery, and it was he who made Sleepy Hollow famous by making it the setting of his tale about the Headless Horseman and Ichabod Crane. Eighty-two years later, in Sleepy Hallow...

March 20, 1962. It was Tuesday—"Thor's Day". The first rays of sunlight were obscured by the dark clouds and rain. Thunder filled the sky, and, every now and then a lightning bolt singed the sky. Inside the hospital, the maternity room was a bustle of activity. A child was scheduled to be born. He was due to come into the world six days earlier, but laziness on his part or something else delayed his arrival, and it was decided to just go in and get him. Dr. Giuseppe Wiseman, OB, was in the delivery room, waiting for his patient to arrive. Since this was to be a cesarean, the anesthesiologist, Dr. Harold Wiseman (no relation) was present, as well as the head nurse, Sarah Wiseman (no relation). As they were waiting for the soon to be mother, Dr. Giuseppe Wiseman, OB, was worried, although he tried not to let it show.

Cesareans were routine procedures, yet this was not a routine patient. A little over a year ago, Wiseman was the

Obstetrician for this same woman, but the delivery ended in tragedy. She had been suffering from an ulcer, and, while she was delivering the ulcer broke. Poison went through the umbilical cord and into the child. He went out to the waiting room to speak to his patient's husband. Having explained the situation, he said, "I will do my best to save them both, but, if I have to save someone, who should it be? Your wife or your child?" The husband, in turn, consulted his pastor, Fr. Dunderhead. Lo, Fr. Dunderhead said unto him, "The rules of Holy Mother Church are quite specific. You must choose the child." The husband thought to himself, and he was not ready to say good-bye to his wife, so he told Dr. Wiseman that, if it comes to one or the other, choose the one. The child born was a girl, named Angelina, but she did not live long. An hour or two. The mother was so sick from all the poison that wen through her body, she was still in the hospital when the child was buried. A wound from which she never recovered.

Indeed, when it came to bearing children, the mother (whose name was Eileen), was not fortunate. The first time she became pregnant, she had a miscarriage. So soon into the pregnancy was it, that she never knew the gender of the child. The next time she was found to be with child, it was winter. One frightful day, she was out shopping. While driving home, another card skid on the ice and crashed into hers. She lost the child. Then, the following year, she was with child again, and it was close to Christmas. She was home, alone, decorating the home and stood on a stool, but she lost her footing and fell, losing the child in the process. Her next pregnancy was Angelina. So, when she learned she was again with child, being a good Irish Catholic, she made a novena to St. Gerard, patron of women who have difficulty in labor.

Now Gerard, who was a tailor and had to cool power to bilocate, is not on record of helping any pregnant women in his lifetime. His life was, rather amazing. An archangel brought him Communion! A statue came to life! Empty pantries were suddenly bursting with bread! Once, a bird came and perched on his finger and sing for a crying child! It was long after his death that he came to to the aid of a pregnant woman.

Italy. 1944. An American soldier just received news from home. It was not good. For three years, he and his wife had been trying to have a baby. Now that his wife was pregnant, complications had set in. Her doctor had given her up hope. It was in this frame of mind that the soldier wandered into the dim-lit Church dedicated to Gerard. Though he had no idea who St. Gerard was, he knelt down before the statue and began to pray: "Good saint of God, help my wife. Help my little baby." He prayed in the Church for a long time. Two days later, he received the cablegram that is now framed in the village church. On the very evening he had knelt before the statue of St. Gerard, across the ocean in a certain American city, his wife happily delivered.

Of course, Dr. Wiseman had no idea that Eileen had made a novena, and such knowledge would have just added to the pressure he was under. He just remembered what happened the last time. Eileen had no ulcers this time, and everything should go by the book. Still...

Outside the hospital, the wind had picked up a bit, and the morning sky was dark. Rain was falling accompanied by thunder and lightning. The thunder was so loud, it could be heard withing the hospital, over all the noise and din that one usually encounters in a hospital.

They were getting ready to bring Eileen into the delivery room, and her husband, whose name shall now be revealed to be George, kissed her and said, "Good luck, honey." He watched as she was leaving, thinking to himself, "What a dumb thing to say." Then it dawned on him that he needed a cigarette, and went to the waiting room and lit one up (hospital rules being somewhat different back then. For one thing, the husband was never in the delivery room. No place for them. It's a job for the professionals).

So Eileen was brought in to the delivery room, where the three Wiseman were waiting. As the anesthesiologist Wiseman administered her spinal, she said a silent prayer and winced. The was a bolt of thunder, which made everyone pause. In the waiting room, George noticed the calendar and laughed to himself. "It's my brother's birthday," he said to no one in particular, and no one listened. Everything was going smoothly, and Dr. Wiseman started to relax a bit. This time, everything will be okay. George, now on his last cigarette, said to himself, "Hey! It's also my niece's birthday." There was another clasp of thunder, when Dr. Wiseman said, "Congratulations! You have a son!" Eileen started crying tears of joy and exclaimed, "Oh, thank you, doctor." Nurse Wiseman spanked the baby to open his lungs and welcome him into the world, and nothing happened. Doctor Wiseman muttered, "Spank him again." Another clasp of thunder, and nothing. Dr. Wiseman was now concerned, and this did not escape Eileen. "Doctor? What's wrong?" From out of nowhere, there was a faint whisper that only Nurse Wiseman could hear. "Solleticare i piedi," it said. "I think we should tickle his feet," she said, and Wiseman nodded. There was another clasp of thunder that was accompanied by the laughter of a newborn. Tuesday's child is full of grace, and on the first day of Spring, in Sleepy Hallow, a mother's prayer was answered.

GENESIS II (SUBSECTION E)

Midnight Mass, 1968.
Holy Innocents Church. Neptune, N.J.

Christmas Eve, 1968. For a little boy growing up on the Jersey Shore, the world was a magical place. This would be his first Midnight Mass, and he was allowed to stay up. The crew of Apollo 8, the first manned mission to the moon, gave a live television broadcast from lunar orbit, in which they showed pictures of the moon and the Earth as seen from the Apollo. He watched with the excitement of a six year old—watched the images and listened as pilot William Anders said, "For all the people on Earth the crew of Apollo 8 has a message we would like to send you—" then each of the astronauts took turns reading the creation account from the Book of Genesis. "In the beginning God created the heaven and the earth…" That night, his mother took him to his first Midnight Mass. Being allowed to stay up so late made him feel very special. Eileen, his baby sister, had only been born only weeks ago, so his sister Mary and his dad remained behind. As they pulled into the parking lot, he noticed all the cars and wondered why there were so many people. As he held his mother's hand, he looked up at the starry sky. He knew that somewhere up there, flying around the moon, there were astronauts. He had never seen so many stars before, mostly because he was usually in bed at this time. On this magical night, as he looked up into the vast beauty of the sky, he thought he felt the breath of God (although some would say it was just the ocean air on a winter night).

As they approached the entrance, he noticed a sign above the door. "You are about to enter the House of God," it read. This was followed by a sentence that would always make him laugh. "Men shall not wear hats." It was not supposed to be funny, but, in his child like mind, he could hear an imposing voice say, "You are about to enter the House of God. Men shall not wear hats," and it just made him laugh. When asked what he was laughing at, he would always respond, "That sign is funny," and people would look at him like he said something weird.

The inside of the Church was brightly lit, decorated, and mobbed. There were old ladies with their rosaries, praying away. They always looked like they were in mourning, and he could never understand why they were so sad. This was a High Mass, which meant there was to be incense. He loved the smell and watched as the smoke gently floated high, and, in his mind, he imagined it was taking up to heaven all the prayers of the people.

He heard the passages from ages ago, and, being a little boy, believed it all without question. The pastor welcomed everyone and gave his homily. He tried to pay attention, but, it was late, and what he had to say had very little meaning to a six year old boy. Still, he had the impression that this night was important, that God was important (even the astronauts knew that), and that he should pay attention, so he did. The bread and wine were brought and the incense was used with great solemnity, and he heard the words, "Through Your goodness we have this wine to offer...," and he wasn't sure why they were offering it to God as he was quite sure God did not eat or drink anything, not having a stomach. Still, he paid attention as best as a six year old boy could at his first Midnight Mass. The Mass moved along. There was more music and more incense, and then everyone sang together, "Holy, Holy, Holy Lord, God of power and might. Heaven and earth are full of your glory. Hosanna in the highest! Blessed is he who comes in the name of the Lord. Hosanna in the highest!' And then everyone fell to their knees. Well, they didn't really fall, but they got down on their knees, and he knew this was something else. Something majestic. Something powerful. After singing such words and everyone on their knees, was God going to be there? In his little boy mind, he knew something big was about to happen.

The priest then said, "And so, Father, we bring you these gifts. Sanctify them by your Holy Spirit to be for your people the Body and Blood of Jesus Christ our Lord." Well, he now knew what the bread and wine were for, sort of. Not really. He did not understand, but, before he could figure it out, the priest said, "On the night he was betrayed He took bread, said the blessing, broke the bread, and gave it to His disciples, and said, "Take this all of you and eat it: This is my Body, which is given for you. Do this in remembrance of Me. After supper, He took the cup, gave thanks, and said, "Drink this, all of you: This is My Blood of the new Covenant, which is shed for you and for many for the forgiveness of sins. Do this in remembrance of Me." When the priest raised the Bread for all to see, bells rang. When he raised the chalice for all to see, bells rang. The little boy took hold of his mommy's hand, for he was very much afraid. He looked behind the priest and saw a huge crucifix, and knew that it was all connected. Gone from his thoughts was Baby Jesus in swaddling clothes. All he saw was the Suffering One, dying horribly.

When it was time for people to receive Communion, he remained quietly in his pew, for he had not yet made his first Communion. He closed his eyes to pray, and they were wet. Had he been crying?

When the Mass had ended, and everyone left in peace to go and love and serve the Lord, his mother asked him how he liked it. He said, "It was scary." As he held his mother's hand, and looked up into the sky, he thought he felt the breath of God, although some would say it was just the ocean air on a cold winter night.

GENESIS III (EXCEPT AFTER "C")

Felt for, he could not be touched.
Looked for, he could not be seen.
Listened for, he could not be heard.
Such are the powers of the Catholic Shaolin Priest.
"Lung Fuel"! The adventures of Kwai Chang Shamolie.

It is 1868 in a small town in the American Old West. Kwai Chang Shamolie is the Catholic Shaolin priest at St. Otto's Mission. Slowly, he walks into town, silently chanting the Office to himself (the Office is a set series of prayers. Morning Prayer. Noon Day Prayer. Evening Prayer and such). He slowly walks by the saloon. Inside, Six Gun, a notorious bad guy, having finished his breakfast, sets to go about his day. Six Gun goes outside, and, as his eyes adjust to the sunlight, he sees the lone figure of Fr. Shamolie. Feeling more nasty than usual, he calls out. "Hey, priest!"

Fr. Shamolie, stops in his tracks. He turns and faces Six Gun, but remains silent.

Six Gun looks at him, smiles, and asks, "If there's a God, why is there so much evil in the world?"

Fr. Shamolie just stand there. He does not say a word, nor does he move.

"I asked you a question, priest!" bellows Six Gun. "Why don't you answer?"

Slowly and softly, Shamolie says, "If you cannot understand my silence. How then, can you understand my words?"

Not sure if he was insulted or not, Six Gun raises his hand and strikes the priest, saying, "You think I'm stupid or something?" Shamolie just stand and stares. Six gun says, "Well? I just struck you. Aren't you going to fight back?"

"I must turn the other cheek," responds Shamolie, slightly bowing.

Six gun removes his gun from his holster and points it at Shamolie. He pulls back the trigger, but his wrist is met by Shamolie's right foot,. The gun flies out of Six Gun's hand, and Shamolie grabs Six Gun's arm, twisting it. Six Gun cries out, "All right! All right! I give up! I give up!"

Shamolie bows and says, "Now, if you excuse me, I will go pray for you to my God." As Shamolie walks back to St. Otto's, he begins to remember when he was a young child, and his training in the Catholic Shaolin monastery. He is a young boy, about eight years old. In front of him is Master Kant, the head of the order. He says to young Shamolie, "You are the one Master (Edgar Allan) Poe calls Weedhopper. Come here, Weedhopper." Shamolie approaches the Master, and Master Kant shows him a closed fist. He opens it and reveals what is inside. "Snatch this cucumber form my hand." Shamolie tries and opens his empty hand, to which Master Kant says, "You missed. Try again." Again he tries and Master Kant says, "You missed. Try again." Young Shamolie tries several times, and each times misses. Finally, Master Kant puts the cucumber down, saying, "You missed, Weedhopper."

Bowing to his venerable Master, Shamolie asks, "Master, what is purpose of that test."

Master Kant smiles and says, "No purpose, Weedhopper. Just make you look silly and make me laugh. Ha! Ha! Ha! Ha! Weedhopper."

Meanwhile, back in the town, Fr. Shamolie is outside the mission door when Six Gun walks by. He calls out to Six Gun, asking, "Six Gun, why is it I do not see you in Church on Sunday?"

Six Gun responds, "Because I'm a Buddhist, priest!"

Shamolie lifts his right leg and kicks Six Gun in the ribs. He then grabs his arm, twisting it behind his back. Six Gun screams, "All right! I'll convert! I'll convert!"

Fr. Shamolie slightly bows, and says, "Now, if you excuse me, I will go pray for you to my God." As Six Gun stumbles away, Shamolie remembers when he was older, and it was time for him to leave the Shaolin monastery. As he was preparing to go, his beloved Master, Master (Edgar Allan) Poe came up to him and said, "Ah, Weedhopper. Before you go, there is one task left. You must pick up the hot, smoldering cauldron and move it from one altar to the next."

Shamolie took a deep bow, said, "Yes, Master," and approached the cauldron. The cauldron was boiling hot. Summing up his powers of concentration, he placed his arms around the cauldron, placed them on the cauldron, and lifted it. Pain swept through his entire body, and he let out an "Arrgh!" Still, he managed to move the cauldron and place it in position on the empty altar. He was blowing on his arms, as he asked,"Master! What was purpose of that test?"

Master Poe was laughing. "No purpose Weedhopper. You were supposed to use the handle! Now you just look silly and make me laugh. Ha! Ha! Ha! Weedhopper. Ha! Ha! Ha! Weeeeeeeedhopppper!"

EXODUS

When we were conceived, we began as a sphere. The ovum. Then, through mitosis, we divided into two cells, and then four (a tetrahedron), then eight (a star tetrahedron), and kept dividing until we got to 512 cells. At that point it forms a toroidal field. A toroidal field is one of the most unique energy fields of the universe, and everything in the universe is based on it. No exception. When the toroidal field keeps growing in the womb, it becomes a human heart. And there's a time when you, I, and everyone else reading this was just a human heart. Before we had hands, feet, head, brain, or anything else, we were a heart. And the heart was beating before we had anything else (Neuroscientists discovered that the heart has its own independent nervous system—a complex system referred to as "the brain in the heart." There are at least forty thousand neurons (nerve cells) in the heart—as many as are found in various subcortical centers of the brain). Then, at a point when it is all developed, the body comes out of the heart, forms the fetus, and pulls the heart into the chest cavity, producing the fetus we are all used to.

In ancient Egypt, when they mummified an important figure, such as a pharaoh, they took the organs in placed them in four clay jars except for two—the brain and the heart. The heart they put back in, because they felt they could not go on to the after life without it. What did they do to the brain? They threw it in the garbage, because it was useless to them.

The teachings of the Vedas understood this. Creation itself began in the heart. The outer world does not actually exist. It is just per consciousness, which appears external, is really internal, created from the heart.

NUMBERS (YOUR DAYS ARE NUMBERS)

"I am so depressed. I just want to die!"

Jesus said that. Yeah. I was surprised, too. I am not being sacrilegious. I am just stating a fact. Jesus said, "I am so depressed. I just want to die." (Matthew 26:38). Depression is NOT a sign of weakness nor was Jesus' depression weak or wrong. In fact, it revealed how deeply he cared for the welfare, not of his own self, but for others. That doesn't mean it was easy for him. He was tempted in every way we are. He was tempted to feel sorry for himself; to become bitter; to seek glory for his work; to neglect his daily responsibilities; to short-cut God's plan. He is sympathetic with our struggles.

Jesus was focused on the suffering of others, and it depressed him. Abraham Lincoln, Jonathan Edwards and David Brainerd were great men who were plagued with life-long melancholy because of their burden to free others from enslavement, punishment or ignorance. The pain of this concern would drive them to bed for weeks. Jesus, too, sought isolation; His compassion for the people would always return him to his responsibility to care for their welfare. He did not shut down. He sacrificed his need for being alone to serve others. Sometimes, it got to him (Matthew 17:17, "How long shall I stay with you? How long shall I put up with you?"). Yet, he did not fly into a bitter tirade about the poor circumstance of his life. He did not create more work for his disciples because he neglected his. Even in the midst of his personal grief, he made life easier for the people near him. This is the lesson of depressed Jesus. His depression did not negate his behavior. It may have motivated it.

At the pinnacle of his anguish in Gethsemane, he cried to his friends,

"I am so depressed. I just want to die!"

He begged them to prayer for him. To his three closest friends, he asked them to just be near him. Yet, they deserted him for sleep, unable to understand what he was going through; unwilling to try. He alone fought the dark dirge engulfing him. So it is with those who are suffering Depression. Many times the suffering individual will finally work up the courage to express the depth of his/her anguish—only to have his/her friends fail to recognize his/her suffering. Agitation, sadness, anxiety, fear—all of it—closing in and the depressed is left to face it alone.

Terrified and astonished at the degree of pain he felt, he collapsed, begging God, "Please, make it stop. You can do anything, you are God."

Troubled, confused, distracted in his emotional travail, he relied on the one truth that shaped his universe, "But its not about me, its about You. I'll do what You ask." I suppose that if he were some sort of superman, he would only have to ask God once and he would have been totally recovered, but he wasn't superman. He was just someone who tried his best to discern and follow the plan God had for him, and now it seemed to be blowing up in his face. First century Palestine did not have modern psychoanalytic theory, nor would it matter much to someone going through depression. Three times he asked God to reconsider, and three times he submitted to the path God designed for him; the path that lead to shame, abandonment and fleeting hell. Even Jesus could not escape depression.

And so it is with those who are suffering depression. Day after day it wears the sufferer down. The depressed battle to navigate through the simplest of tasks. They struggle to just keep moving, to keep one foot in front of the other. The struggle is almost all-consuming. It is dark. It is frightening. It is scary. It is worrisome. It is depressing. Their cries to God seem to go unheeded at times. God is distant. God is a tormentor. God is...depressing.

Jesus wrestled through the loneliness, the frustration of lack of communication, the lack of comfort and the strong desire to end the situation in some way that would be more appealing than the cross and facing his Father's wrath. He had to work through it. He was not immune to it. He wrestled and struggled and scratched and clawed, fighting temptation, and submitted to his Father's plan and purpose. Those who suffer with Depression go through the same thing—but they can work through it all and realize that this suffering will eventually produce good. They will not enjoy the situation, and it may indeed get worse. But they have hope. Jesus can identify with the depressed. The depressed can identify with Jesus. Jesus battle with depression seems to be life long (he did not just suffer it at Gethsemane). Jesus was depressed. He is victorious. But enough of my ramblings

DIETER ROAMING

Man at his best, like water,
Serves as he goes along:
Like water he seeks his own level,
The common level of life,
—Lao Tzu—Chapter 8, Tao Te Chang

A Benedictine monk is in the school of the Lord's service. What does it mean to be in a student in the school of the Lord's service? St. Benedict makes it clear in his rule. To serve the Lord, we must serve each other. But why? Why did we come to this school? Why did we enroll? Why choose a Benedictine school? What does it mean to be a student in a school run by those who consider themselves to be students in the Lord's service?

St. Benedict knew that one of the basic truths is that before you can change the world you've got to change yourself. We cannot relieve suffering while we are bound to the emotions that create suffering. If we work for peace with fear and hatred in our hearts, we will be confounded. If we teach morality without learning to control our cravings, we will succeed only in teaching cynicism. In order to foster wisdom in others, we must develop it in ourselves.

Meditation, prayer, and lectio divina helps us to see the world and ourselves more clearly (lectio divina, or "divine reading," is a form of meditation on the Scriptures associated with the Benedictines). It is a tool for cutting through the fog of delusion. Through these tools we develop mindfulness, which allows us to be more aware of our thoughts, emotions, and responses. Seeing through delusion we become aware of the unity and interdependence of all things. We see our relationship to the whole of life. The illusion of separateness disappears. When we get up from prayer we hope to carry with us into the rest of our lives the clarity and right intention we've attained while sitting. This requires the practice of holding awareness as we go about our lives. When we are mindful of our actions, we see more clearly the effects of our behavior. We come to understand how our thoughts and behavior affect our moods and how they affect other people.

It is helpful to have guidelines for living a thoughtful and connected life. For this, Benedict gives us his little Rule for beginners.

This is all very well, but what does this mean for us, the student? Think of the first day of school, or rather, shortly before the first day. You are out school shopping. You get things your mother thinks you need, but you do not. You get things you say you need, but do not. Then you get things you actually need. You come to school quite loaded down, and you have yet to acquire all the books you will need throughout the year, which will only increase your load. Before you can begin to be a student, you must ask, what am I carrying that others tell me I need, what am I carrying that I thought I needed, and what do I actually need? You will see that your burden will be lighter—and will no longer be a burden.

Our minds are working all the time. We are sensing, perceiving, remembering, interpreting, regulating body processes, refocusing attention, planning, willing, and acting moment by moment. As we go about our activities, we tend to be unaware of most of our mental activity. Generally, that's

OK, because living is a complex process, and it's best that we focus that sliver of brain activity we call consciousness on the most urgent business at hand. If things are going well, that inner director of consciousness will focus our awareness on what is important. We will then make appropriate choices and feel productive. Life will seem meaningful and worthwhile.

Sometimes life throws too much at us, and the part of our mind that directs our focus becomes overwhelmed. We may find ourselves attending exclusively to the practical matters of survival, and losing touch with the more subtle experiences of our inner thoughts and emotions. Sometimes that inner director works as a censor or guard and directs attention away from areas of mental activity that seem too dangerous or painful. Big hunks of life activity can fall out of our awareness, because the focusing or directing component of consciousness has decided we're not going to deal with that.

When we have been wounded, our mind will have develop a strategy for managing situations where we might be wounded again. It may tell us that when this kind of danger arises, we're going to run away, either literally or by taking away awareness. It may decide that anger is the best defense, or maybe humor or seductiveness or being a bully will make things safe. Sometimes we don't really have much of a strategy for dealing with our hurts, so we just become confused.

We may have learned the strategy of thinking through problems, and try to apply that to problems where we don't have all the data, perhaps because the problem is still in the future. So we worry. Not being able to solve the problem, but sticking to our strategy, we worry some more. We can keep this up for a long time Some people never stop. The price worriers pay is that their mental resources are focused on problems without solutions, and they don't have much left for the rest of life. Being productive and enjoying the experience of living are sacrificed to the obligation to fret.

None of us wants to be the victim of misdirected awareness or of a faulty strategy for allocating mental resources. We'd rather be effective in our thinking and doing. We'd rather have emotions that fit circumstances now, than emotions that reflect past experience that may be similar, but different in some key way. When our emotions are fresh and authentic and our thinking is flexible, our behavior is more spontaneous, and our experience is rich.

Mindfulness is a practice that helps us expand the scope of awareness. It allows awareness to stay with us in the now. When we are mindful we are more likely to respond genuinely to circumstances. We are more aware of emotions and can interpret them more accurately. Meditation is a primary tool for developing the skill of mindfulness.

So now we are not just students of students in the school of the Lord's service. We are students who are Mindful—Mindful of ourselves, and of our brother students. Why is this? Because deep in our hearts, we heard His voice, no matter how we conceive Him to be (Jew, Christian, Muslim, Buddhist, Hindu, etc.). Deep in our hearts, we felt His Presence. Deep in our hearts, we were loved. We were loved into existence. We were loved as we went along our way. We are loved at this very moment, and we are so filled with love that we cannot contain it. It has to be shared. Demands to be shared. So we come to this school of the Lord's service, to learn how to share that love—how to serve one another. To do that, we must be present for one another.

How difficult it can be to be fully present for another person. In the Gospel story of the events following the Last Supper, while Jesus is experiencing the pain of his unfolding betrayal,

He asks the apostles to stay awake with him and pray, but they all fall asleep. He asks them several times to be awake with him, but each time they fall asleep.

It is a touching and telling story of the frailty of these saints, future Church fathers, evangelists. Even they had trouble being awake in the presence of another's pain. It is not unnatural to withdraw our attention when someone is hurting. It is unhelpful, however.

One of the characteristics of an effective counselor is that they stay present in the counseling session. If the therapists mind is somewhere else, they are not much help to the client. Similarly, when relationships fail, it is often the case that one or both of the partners has a pattern of withdrawing attention. How often has the counselor heard, "He/She does not listen to me"?

The emotions of aversion keep us from making contact with people in their need. We may fear that their pain will become our pain. We may fear they will get too close, if they get too close they may see the dark truth about us. They may see our weakness and inadequacy. They may not like what they see. Instead of getting close, we may become nervous, distracted, bored. We may remember some other pressing commitment that we just have to take care of right now.

Being mentally and emotionally present with another person is one of the best gifts we can give. It is calming and healing. It creates connection and intimacy. It opens emotional doors. It is how we serve one another.

Some rare people are able to be fully present with others quite naturally. Most of us have to develop that capacity. Some of the qualities we need are self-awareness, self-acceptance, and compassion. The ability to understand and move beyond our aversions comes from self-awareness. Compassion grows out of self-acceptance. The intention to listen—to be present—grows out of compassion. St. Benedict knew this. This is why he begins his rule by stating we must listen with the ear of our heart.

These qualities we can grow in ourselves. Through practice of meditation, prayer, and lectio we can become more self-aware. Through self-awareness and consciously being kind to ourselves we can become more self-accepting As we work through our distaste for the darkness in our own hearts we become more able to open our hearts to others. When we open our hearts to others we can be with them in their pain and in their joy.

When you face a challenge, make a mistake, get up in the morning, do your work, or just sit there doing nothing, what is your internal commentary? All of us talk to ourselves as we go through the day. Most of us keep it quiet, internal, largely out of awareness, but the self-talk helps us frame our experience. It connects the immediate experience with our past. It fits the moment into our belief system. It also influences our response to situations.

When we are self-critical and negative, we are less likely to succeed than if we are encouraging to ourselves and positive. The commentary influences the outcome of the episode. It shapes our experience.

When you trip over an obstacle, does your internal voice say, "I'm clumsy"?

When you make a mistake, do you say to yourself, "I'm stupid"?

When you face a challenge, do you tell yourself, "What if I fail? It'll be a catastrophe."

Such thoughts will be accompanied by unpleasant emotion. They make us feel bad, and they reinforce negative beliefs about the world and ourselves.

If you want a certain type of experience, a certain type of outcome in your life, you had best be aware of what you are saying to yourself. If you constantly berate yourself, or tell yourself to expect the worst, you can hardly expect to feel good.

To remedy our bad self-talk habits we must be aware of the chatter. We tune in. Then simply change the content of the monologue to something more loving, encouraging, optimistic.

This can be tricky, because we can pack a lot of emotion and meaning into a short word or phrase. When we tell ourselves we are stupid or unlovable or a failure, we likely have a long string of memory associations with the comment. The memories probably go back to early childhood when we started to form our beliefs about the world and ourselves. You may not be able to change the memory, but you can alter the associations. You can choose to develop the habit of using self-talk that doesn't bring up your negative mental baggage. Instead you can encourage and nurture yourself

"God so loved the world that He gave His Son." Jesus is our gift from God. This is the most precious Gift that we will ever receive, and, through the Eucharist, we can receive Him daily. Would God give us this Gift if He did not value us so highly? If God can love us tins much, can we not love ourselves?

In order to be friends with someone, one must first know how to be primarily one's true self in all its wholeness. Being whole is in itself a gift, like faith, something innately ours if we are open to it.

The love we have for one another has long seemed to be one of the most important and desirable things in life, It is a bundle of many things—partly romance but partly everyday practicality, giving but also getting, trusting but also being trusted, taking care of and being taken care of. Even more, it is the sharing of experiences, of hopes, of fears, of pleasures, of sorrows, Above all, it gives, as its greatest gift to each individual, a feeling of belonging and a sense of completeness.

Often in today's world, we are raised with the idea that we are not innately gifted with wholeness, but that we come into this world unwhole or unholy. The messages we may receive as we journey through life confirm our unholiness rather than the opposite. The question, "What is wrong with you?" that we hear as children is one example.

A change of mindset can change the way we perceive ourselves, others, and the world around us. Thinking of ourselves as blessings, for example, rather than as sinners, can greatly influence our attitudes and actions for the better,

There is a story told about a woman who found herself standing on the edge of a cliff, petrified by fear of plunging to her death, until a kindly monk walked by and suggested she take three steps back and change her perspective. Like her, we too can change our perspectives.

Take time today to change your perspective with regard to yourself and the people around you by thinking of yourself and others as blessings put on this earth by God. Think of what it means to you to be a blessing, and come up with ways you would imagine a blessing would act toward family members, friends, co-workers, enemies, and strangers. Make these ways your traveling companions, and take them out and share them with others through your actions as often during the day as you can.

You are serving another by giving your true self, and your true self is a blessing. When you catch yourself doing this, you will also realize you're being a friend.

The school of the Lord's service requires that we serve others, and we will serve them in times of joy and in times of distress. Among all people, one who loves will not leave. God is Love and the source of love. His love is unending and constantly filling. Thus, love cannot know the measure of its depth until the hour of parting.

Grief is the emotion that fills the empty space in our hearts left by the loss of a loved one. When we love a person or thing and it passes away we naturally feel loss. Sadness and tears come to mark the loss. They signal to us and those around us that a significant event has occurred, and that we may need aid in our mourning.

When we cry, we are a veritable multimedia show in non-verbal communication. The tear, streaming and reflective, catches the light and signals that something emotionally significant is happening. Our face reddens, as it would if we couldn't breathe, showing that we need to be attended to. As we sob, we express a sound not unlike a baby's wail, the supreme attention getter, and our body moves rhythmically and distinctively in the sobbing, so that even from a distance, a companion may see that all is not well. The act of crying is a magnificently designed signal of human need. Each change in a person's appearance while crying naturally pulls in the attention of those around them. Just as humans are equipped to cry, we have built-in inclinations to respond to crying by offering comfort.

In the best of bad situations, we would experience a loss and respond to it by crying. Someone near us would pickup the signal of our pain and come to our aid. In their closeness, their touch, and gentle reassurance we would be reminded that we are not alone, that we will be supported in our emotional readjustment.

Unfortunately, it doesn't always go that way. Culture sometimes interferes with the natural way of things. Culture may tell us it is not appropriate to show our emotions or respond to others in the comforting that would be so natural. Living and working in cities we are less likely to be surrounded by a close group of intimates whose roles include responding to our emotional needs.

Instead of experiencing our emotional pain, being comforted, and moving on with life, we modems are prone to pushing our emotions away, keeping a stiff upper lip, and adopting an appearance that nothing is wrong. We may even fool ourselves into believing that our deep losses should not be felt. We harden ourselves, so that the pain doesn't show. We lose contact with our emotions, and as we do, we lose some of our ability to respond as God intended. Remember, even Jesus cried at Lazarus tomb. If God can cry, then who are we to hold our emotions back?

Grieving is emotional healing. If we are unable to grieve our losses, we have difficulty moving on. We forfeit some of our emotional flexibility. Our psyches develop hard spots, and these may manifest themselves in habitual anger, irritability, anxiety, depression, or addiction.

One of the great universal truths is that all things must pass. Loss is inevitable. People come into our lives, and sometimes they go out of our lives. Sometimes the going is in the form of death. It is neither fair nor unfair; it is just the nature of life.

Life includes dying, Sadness is natural when a loved one dies. It is healthy to mourn, to feel the emotion of such a loss.

It is also natural that the sadness lessens in time. We must be able to let it go when it has run its course.

If we are to allow joy into our lives, we must be able to grieve our losses. To do that, we need to be able to feel the emotion. It is helpful to have someone to talk to about the losses. A sympathetic companion can be comforting and can help us gather perspective that can be hard to come by in the state of grief

Touch base with your heart. What emotions are you having? Look there for the seed of compassion. Let it grow. Let your heart open. Look there for the emotion you may have known in a special moment with a loved one. This is an emotion of comfort and warmth. Feel this warm and comfortable emotion and imagine that it is a brilliant light in your heart. It is Light—the Light—for God is Love.

Let this Light grow in your heart. Let it grow so that it fills you up and fills the entire room. Remind yourself that love and compassion are limitless and that they fill the universe.

Imagine that the Love of the universe is a Light that shines on you and upon the person you are sitting with. Let the Love shower you with light and empower your spirit. See yourself as a conduit for all the love and compassion in the world, which you channel to this other person. Become the branch of the vine! See the Light shining in your heart flowing through you to the other. Feel the compassion and loving kindness in you and in the entire world flowing from you to them. God is Love, and His supply is limitless, so you need not be depleted.

Love is like a chain. It is only as strong as its weakest link. It is the spaces within a chain that make it useful and give it strength. So we must listen for the spaces between us, giving each other the space to grow and to become who we were meant to be. We nurture each other by filling these spaces with love.

Love is patient. Love is kind. Love is harmony, even in discord. To know Love, be like a running brook, which deaf, yet sings its melodies for others to hear. Feel the pain of too much tenderness. Awake each day with a winged heart and give thanks to God for another day of loving.

To love is to be vulnerable. To love is to know pain. To love is to no longer live for ourselves but for another. Love demands not only a great detachment from self-centeredness but also a strenuous carrying of the cross. It is a pearl of great price, and, with God's help, we are willing to pay that price, and that is what brings us to the school of the Lord's service. That is why we enrolled as students, That is why we are here today. We were loved into existence, we are loved at this very moment, and we are present here as students of students in the school of the Lord's service.

LEVI T. CUSS

I'm standing at the entrance of the abyss
A blanket of darkness covers the sky
And once shiny white clouds
Fade away like the rain
The wind is violent
Poison has filled the air
Yet I stand unwavering
Waiting…
What lies in the void?
Why does it wish to devour
Everything?
I'm not the enemy nor is it mine
I'm just standing in between
Life and death
I suppose I'm the thing holding "it"
And "it" holding me
But like I said
This is not my enemy

The other day I came home from work after midnight. The cats were lounging on the couch. I said to them, "Come on, guys! When I come home and it's the witching hour, I expect something to be brewing in the pot!' They looked at me with an expression that read, "Why are you talking to us like that for?' this is because I hardly talk to the cats in English (and, when I do, I usually use a foreign accent or my New Jersey accent).

Instead, I speak to them in a series of clicks, much like Xi in the highly recommended "the Gods Must Be Crazy" (and the not so highly recommended "The Gods Must Be Crazy II). So I repeated myself in clicks, adding that I expected them to "do something witchy." I forgot that Charles Manson once told his followers to do just that when they broke into peoples homes. We had been watching a documentary on Manson the other night, and, although they could not understand a word, I caught them reading the subtitles and glancing at each other knowingly. Today, I came home from work after midnight. I noticed Folgers crystals were spilled outside the door. When I went inside, all the furniture had been rearranged. "Holter Skelten" was spelled in ketchup on the fridge (So they misspelled it. They're cats, for crying out loud). I wiped a tear from my eye. I was so proud of them.

> See no body and see no mind.
> Yet within thine bending sickle's compass stilting choking,
> the anxiety pawns your mind
> And why they do, to me, it's certainly baffling.
> So I wrapped it around the back of a chair
> And before I knew it,
> I fell into the cloudy yesterdays of my mind
> that feeds on turbulent emotions in stillness of air
> while the circumcised wren burbles gently
> gently licking the salt from a pork rind, I silently watch defiantly
> For the mind is nameless unrecognizable
> as the head that was shorn
> nor can we all just regress,
> into the nothingness to which we are no less?
> A western wind has just been born
> There is no enlightenment to experience

"Hello," was all I could muster to say
with nine lives a kitten dies but once
opens windows, opens doors
This is called liberation.
Would my refusal get me any further,
from where I have already been?
Never mind I am still lost in confusion
I'm never going to be what I've been.

~~~~~~

I am Otto L. Penquist, and all my life I've had a dream. I had always wanted to bleed. To bleed without purpose would not serve me nor anyone; but to bleed, to become a phlebotomist, and to serve others doing so was my greatest dream. How was one to go about this? One could not very well say, "Hey, how about a vivisection?" Answer: The Blood Mobile!

Now my dream would be fulfilled. Accompanied by my friend, Jim Porto, we went off to give blood. Jim, a frequent blood donor, seemed quite happy about what laid ahead. He was singing, "I'm gonna give blood, I'm gonna give blood, I'm gonna give blood." What was his obsession in blood? Then I remembered, he played Renfield in "Dracula." In fact, one write-up said he played the role with "some credibility." This thought crept in my mind and kept echoing. Then Jim looked at me with what seemed to be an evil gleam in his eye and said, "Time to go."

We arrived at the desk, and Jim said in a low voice, "Follow me, lad. I'll create a diversion while you get a needle and ram it in me. Got It?"

I said in reply, "Why don't we just fill out the forms?"

"Sure, act natural, just like one of them. Who would suspect? You're a genius kid," he responded.

We then had our temperatures taken. The nurses whispered something to each other and insisted on using rectal thermometers. We proceeded to comply when something flashed, it looked amazingly like a camera, but the nurses said it was a new type of X-ray and we checked out. Jim turned red, I was confused, but off we went for the blood test. I scored an A + which wasn't bad as I didn't see any questions. Some people were getting 0's; now that's low. We then went off to the tables where people were lying down to give blood. It was quite painless, which upset Jim who was yelling, "Put the needle in deeper! I want pain, do you hear me, pain!"

When it was over, Jim inquired on when he could do it again. Then we sat down. The place where we sat down was surrounded by a number of free gifts. Jim said, "People shouldn't give blood for the gifts, but because they want to." He then took a mug, a Frisbee, a patch, a bumper sticker, and a brownie.

It was over, and I had accomplished my dream. There were some people who wouldn't give. Excuses were, "I drink too much orange juice and have acid blood," "I gave at the office," and a variety of others, but I knew the real reason. Then there were the brave souls who gave for the first time, only to be disappointed because they didn't die like they were told they would by those who never gave in their life.

College—what is it? Is it not a place where young adults go to prepare for the future? Whatever decisions that they make will be carried by them the rest of their lives. Are not these young adults also the future of the U.S.A.? Then these young students must become responsible for their daily

lives upon graduating. What if some fiendish world-power was to interfere with America's education of those who shape her future? Through painstaking efforts and cutthroat tactics, we have found evidence of such devious activity. Where? Where do people go when then need information on research papers and other such educational novelties? The libraries, that's where. What if the books in the library were to be replaced by exact duplicates, only with key sentences changed to subvert the reader? How could this be done? By replacing student librarians with spies surgically altered to look exactly like a typical student librarian. This is the shocking story of how it came about.

Enter Baron Von Entwistle, simply known as the Baron. It was he who presented the idea to his government, but the idea was not originally his. In fact, when he was first presented with the idea he scoffed at it as being absurd, and it wasn't until he was offered money that he wholeheartedly and unhesitatingly agreed. The one who came up with the actual idea of subverting the American youth was the mysterious Mr. N. He met the Baron in an alley by a bar. Disguised as a wino, Mr. N. told the Baron of his idea. The only problem was how to put the idea into a working operation. Mr. N. found his old physics teacher, professor Malcolm.

Professor Malcolm came up with what became know as the "the plan," Simply stated, "the plan" was to surgically alter master spies, train them on the Dewey Decimal System, plant them in a small college in the U.S.A., and have the spies switch books with the duplicate ones. A small college was chosen because everyone knows everyone by sight, if not by name, and people might tell other people about the exciting book they just read, unaware that they are being subliminally corrupted. The Baron, having been paid well by Mr. N., received permission of his government to train two top master spies; Eddy Mology and Gene Alogy. Disguised as stamps, they were mailed to the U.S.A.

"The plan" would have gone over well, except for one thing. The fact was that these student librarians were too perfect, too well organized, and even had names that were too innocent; names like "Joy" and "Tammy" just seemed too American to us (that is Mr. Penquist and I). Why could these two students not present a birth certificate or even a passport on demand like any normal American? We knew something was up, and that a foreign power must be involved. Take, for example, the book, "A Tale of Two Cities, by Charles Dickens; the opening sentence should read, "It was the worst of times, it was the best of times," not "It was a time to overthrow the government and then blow ourselves up.

The End." Everyone should know that a novel consists of more than two sentences. What about the library security devise, the turnstile? Can it also be X-raying our pockets or transmitting secret plans to enemy satellites orbiting the Earth? Where do the overdue library book fines go? Perhaps to other no-good nicks up to no good? Why do books have to be stamped? Perhaps there is something in the ink that only a selected few are able to see. In any case, the most obvious question here is being ignored, and that is with theories like mine, why am I allowed to roam the streets? Are they scared to put me, away? Maybe I'll find out something I should not know, or maybe, just maybe, I'm right.

SECURITY TREKNET

Saint Otto College: the matriculant frontier. These are the voyages of the Saint Otto Security Team. It's ongoing mission: to explore strange new dorms, to seek out college criminal activity, to boldly arrest those never arrested before.

Squad Leader Captain's Log; Saint Otto date March 8. This is the campus of Saint Otto College. My name is Quirk. I'm a security officer. I'm a cop (dum de dum dum).

I was sitting in my office dreaming of my secretary when the call came. It was a disturbance outside of the theatre, (dum de dum dum). My right hand man Mr. Stock and I went to check it out, (dum de dum dum, dummmm). We arrived at 6:30 p.m. There was someone waiting for us. I recognized him right away it was the mysterious Triple B, (dum dum dum). He was by the fountain outside the theatre. He seemed upset. We checked it out, (dum de dum dum).

"You called us?" I asked as we showed him our badges.

"Yes," he replied. "Someone stole the fish that was in this fountain." (dum dum dum).

"Fascinating!" remarked Mr. Stock. I proceeded to question Triple B.

"Give me the facts. Just the facts."

"Alright. I was setting up lights for play rehearsal—"

"Play? What play?" I asked.

He replied, "Sound of Music" (dum dum dum).

"When and where is it being done?" I asked. "From March 17th-20th at the local roundabout theatre." "Alright, go on."

"I was setting up lights when I heard a splash from outside. I went out to check what happened and noticed that the grass around the fountain was wet. That's when I noticed that the fish was gone, and then I called you."

"Stock, I have a hunch, it's just a hunch, that someone stole the fish," I said.

"I would say that was a logical assumption," replied Mr. Stock.

"Thank you for your help Triple B,. We'll ask around," I said. We then left, (dum de dum dum).

We were walking towards the student center when a call came over my walky-talky.

"Spott to Captain! Spott to Captain!"

"Quirk here."

"Captain, I was going over the engines in the security cars. In security car #1 the carburetor is generating excess matter, if it continues at this rate, I canna be responsible for the safety of the car ""Calm down, Spotty."

"Ach! The car is going to blow itself to pieces!"

"I want answers, Mister!"

"Well I tried stickin' a potatoe up the tailpipe, but it didina do a bit o'good."By the by, you wouldn'a "Analysis, Stock?"

"It would appear that Mr. Spott is about is out one potatoe."

"Logical, totally logical; however, I was referring to the problem with the car engine."

"I would suggest that the car be lent out only to people from the college newspaper, that way if the car blows up, the paper would never be printed, and anarchistic garbage would never be read."

"But I like the opinions column."

"The needs of the many outweigh the needs of the few. Anyway, logic would dictate that the only reason you like the

Opinions Column is, like any book you read, it has to have pictures."

"As always your logic is impeccable, Mr. Stock."

"Spott here, Captain."

"Mr. Snott, let that car out for the college newspaper use only."

"Aye, Captain. It will be my pleasure."

With that he signed off, (dum de dum dum).

"Come, Mr. Stock, let us be on our way," (dum de dum dum, dummm).

7:07 p.m.—We arrive at the Student Center. "Fascinating!" said Stock.

"What is it Stock?"

"Look over by the 'Star Castle' video game machine Captain." Stock was right, the sight was fascinating. A young woman was standing by the machine (dum dum dum).

"I must question her." We went over to her and showed her our badges. "Excuse me, Miss, Security. Mind answering a few questions?"

She replied, "Guys are rocks, rocks don't talk, I don't talk to guys."

"What does that mean?"

"Captain, I believe she is in the midst of some ritual called 'pledging.' It is forbidden for her to talk to any male."

"Wait a minute, Stock. We make the laws around here."

"Captain, are you forgetting the Prime Directive?"

"Don't I always?"

"Captain, there are some things that transcend the discipline of security."

"Where does that leave us?"

"Captain, I would suggest the mind meld."

"Go to it, Stock."

Stock placed his fingers on the forehead of the young woman and said, "Your mind is my mind, our thoughts are one." After the mind meld, I talked with Stock.

"Stock, what happened?"

"She has a very high I.Q., Jim, in fact, she's a very beautiful person. Gorgeous even. Why, I'd even go so far as to say—"

"Hold it Stock,! I get the girl here. It's in the contract."

"She's not for you, Jim."

"That's also in the contract. Anyway, what about the fish?"

"She doesn't know anything about it."

"Great," I sighed. "Let's press on," (dum de dum dum, dummmm).

After eight hours of discussing who might have been responsible for the fishnapping, we narrowed it down to two leads. It was then 3:00 a.m., (dum de dum dum). We went home to continue the next day, (dum du dum dum, dummmm).

Squad Leader Captain's Log: Saint Otto date March 9. At 1:15 p.m. we were back on the case, (dum de dum dum). At 1:32 p.m. we arrive at the Fisherman's room (an actor of extraordinary acting, juggling, and vaudevillian talent. Too bad he can't sing).

"You Fisherman?" I asked. "Saint Otto Security." I said as I showed him my badge.

"Yeah, I guess I am. What do you want?"

"Do you know anything about the missing fish Triple B reported?"

"Triple B! he exclaimed.

"Anything wrong with him?" I asked.

"Yeah, I'll tell you what's wrong with him. He gets the girls. He always gets the girls! In fact, he's so lucky his own roommate is contemplating the priesthood."

"Captain!" yelled Stock, "I smell fish" (dum de dum dum).

"I have cans of tuna, that's all," said the Fisherman.

"Sorry, Stock," I said, "But we're looking for a bass," (dum de dum dum, dummmm). With that Stock gave Fisherman his famous neck pinch.

"Kinky," said the Fisherman as he passed-out, (dum dum dum).

2:15 p.m. Stock and I went to see the movie, Herpie the Love Bug Goes to College, (dum de dum dum).

4:30 p.m. Thanks to informants Rodney and Juan and their pet rock Eric, I found out the name of lead number two to be Kristy, (dum de dum dum, dummmm). I knew that she had no information about the fish-napping, but she's very beautiful so it couldn't hurt. I went alone. The interrogation lasted eleven days.

Squad Leader Captain's Log: Saint Otto date March 19. I arrived at the office at 12:06 p.m., (dum de dum dum). "Anything on that fish case, Stock?"

"No, Captain," I decided to call in the God Squad (the leaders of the campus ministry). Their leader was Linc Moe Lee." Linc came in followed by Pogostick Jim who kept singing, "Follow Moe Lee. Follow Moe Lee."

"How can I help?" he asked.

"We are at a loss in this case. We need some divine help," said Stock.

"We'll get on it right away," said Linc, (dum de dum dum).

After 200,000 Paternosters, Linc returned. "Have you checked the fountain again?"

"No, that's where it was stolen from."

"Wrong," said Linc, "It was revealed to me in a nocturnal vision this afternoon that Otto Penquist removed the fish to give it a bath and later put it back."

"Oh, come on, that's rather far fetched," I said.

"Blame the author of this piece, not me. Anyway, the fish is back."

On March 20, Otto Penquist was arraigned, indicted and convicted of removing a fish for a bath without notifying anyone and for doing so out of season. The crime of bathing fish out of season is punishable by no less than 15 hours of elevator music.

The story you just read is 99 44/100% pure fantasy and everything was changed to protect the author.

Downstairs in the Student Center of St. Otto University is the headquarters for the Secret Government Agents, or S.G.A. Their plan, to infiltrate and destroy all of the Fruit-of-the-Loom factories, has always been thwarted by the Criminal Underhanded Bureau, or C.U.B., as they're called; As this semester began, C.U.B. was leaderless and lay in general anarchy. This was a perfect time for the S.G.A. to wipe out the enemy.

The S.G.A. chose from among themselves Agent P—the most dreaded agent of all ! An agent that once seduced a nation and remembered all of their names ! With Agent P on the job, how could C.U.B. survive?

Luckily, although C.U.B. was leaderless, it was not defenseless. It had Agent Miami M. Here was a man who would spend a half hour searching in his driveway for his car, which was parked in the street all the time. (This became known as Project Nick). Why choose him? Because he had the total and complete confidence of James Watt, and could obtain at any time a thermonuclear device, using the excuse that he wanted to kill squirrels. More important was Miami M's friendship with Otto Penquist, an influential, if somewhat short, Junior. However, Agent P knew this and was determined to seduce, if not kill Otto (let it be known that Agent P is a girl and Otto is no fruit, so there).

Fearing for his friend's safety, Miami M went to Watts' headquarters and found Special K. Special K is a sinister left-handed genius who once was disguised as a traveler's check in the famed

Maudlin case (now available on cassette for $8.95 from Penquist Productions, Ltd.,). Special K's mission was to get to Otto before Agent P did, and to protect Otto from harm.

Otto, of course, was unaware of all this. Spending most of his time in the Student Center giving dissertations on the value of Creating All New Dental Instruments (or Candi). Otto blissfully spent his existence, and quarters, pretending to destroy the universe on Destructo—the ultimate video game. When he wasn't doing that, he could be found writing a research paper on crop dusters, tentatively titled "Mary Ellen" (no one knows why).

Then came what would later be called "Tuesday," in the annals of spy history (although it was really Wednesday). This day was like any other day for Otto. He was still playing Destructo when Agent P came up to him. She asked him seductively, "Want to see my tokens?"

Suddenly, Special K appeared! Realizing the danger, K said, "Those aren't real tokens, they're falsies!"

Sensing things were getting tense, Otto tried to calm things down, "Anyone read the paper? Miami M was elected leader of C.U.B."

"What? They have a leader?" exclaimed Agent P. "This changes the whole situation." With that, she left.

"I guess I'm no longer needed," said Special K, and she, too, left (didn't know K was a girl, did you?). So Otto, not realizing his life had been in jeopardy, destroyed the Starship Pleeble and put another token in the machine.

Why? (Nov. 1984)

Sitting in the corner of
a rainy afternoon,
Watching the yellow and red
rubber blobs,
listening to the echo
of a faded dream.
The grayness of the sky
mirrors my soul
and the clouds are shedding
the tears behind my eyes.
The light is gone and
the shadows are all that is left.
The morning papers herald
that the children suffered unto Him slaughtered like a paschal lamb
and the mist that rises
from the streets
is no longer accompanied
by their laughter.
I am dark.

Somewhere in the bowels of Saint Otto University lurks the most dreaded fear of all students. The upper-classmen are aware and take caution, but for freshmen caught unawares, it can turn their life into a living Hell! This is the story of one of them—Kim Gorgeous! Freshmen at large!

Kim Gorgeous had an assignment for which she had to do research, and so she decided to use the library. Unknown to her, the library was having troubles. In the summer the library was supposed to break ground for expansion. This new library would have contained books by great thinkers from all over the world. Tests were created, programs were formulated, and all kinds of methods for storing the Dewey Decimal System were devised. Then someone said, "Where are we going to get the money for all this?" That simple question has no simple answer and the result is that the current library is in four buildings; the library, St. Frank Hall, the old gym and a room in Saint Otto Hall. The upper classmen know that they may have to go through all four of these buildings before finding the material they want; freshmen are unprepared. So Kim went off to the library in perfect bliss (as ignorance creates).

Her first obstacle was getting in the library. She went up the doors and pushed, but they wouldn't open. She tried pushing again, but no luck. No matter how hard she tried she couldn't get in, and, she was about to give up, she read the sign on the door. It said, "Pull."

Next came the much feared security turnstile. Many terrorist groups were denied access to the inner chambers thanks to this handy devise. Legend has it that famed secret agent Patrick Edwards was caught with a heat-seeking missile in his binder (at the time he was undercover as a student). Now Kim Gorgeous had to face the turnstile. She looked at it carefully, I.D. in hand, and then suddenly she stopped dead in her tracks. She wondered where she had to put her I.D. in order for the turnstile to work, but there was no slot for the I.D. Did she dare just walk right through and hope that the turnstile didn't think her a Soviet agent? She waited to see what other students did, and Otto Penquist, a Junior, came in and went right through with no problems. Understanding for the first time that the turnstile doesn't take I. D.s, she went in and proceeded to the card catalog.

Finding the book that she needed listed in the catalog, she went to go find it. The book, "The Six Year Old and His Philosophy," was listed as PU 3.2062. Having trouble finding the PU section, she went and asked the librarian for assistance. The Librarian, whose vast superior intelligence spans the history of man, was quick to reply that the book was in one of the three other places. The librarian then said that Kim could pick up the book the next day. Alas, Kim put off getting the book until the last minute, so she did the next best thing—she panicked. Getting an imperial writ from the Librarian, Kim Gorgeous went to search for her book.

First Kim went to Saint Frank Hall but, after several hours of looking, PU 3.2062 was not there. Next, she went to Saint Otto Hall, but to no avail. Soon she became delirious as the walking took it's toll. Everything looked like a book. When she finally arrived at her destination, she was near death. The book she needed was not there. She knew not what to do; she was exhausted and feverish. As she was roaming the campus she heard a loud scream.

Several groupies had just seen Eddie C, the campus actor extraordinaire, and they couldn't contain themselves. Having noticed Kim moping about, Eddie, asked her her problem. Fortunately for Kim,

Ed had read "The Six Year Old and His Philosophy," and, using his extraordinary actors' mind, recited, to her word for word the entire book that very night.

So what started out a living Hell for a freshmen turned out alright in the end. A small scholastic lesson from the campus of Saint Otto University.

Spring Semester loomed large on the horizon and that meant it was time to register for the upcoming semester. Soon the schedules were out and the advisors were prepared for the upcoming onslaught of eager inquiring minds whose quest for an authoritative signature on their student course selection form is second only to their desire to find the funds for next semester's tuition. The people at Records thought they would have a giggle by having a computer print the schedule and at the same time blinding the students when they attempted to read it. Several of the students' optic nerves shorted out and one student went insane. A very large majority of the male population came out of records depressed when they realized that the females who work there are married.

All students are different, and, therefore, have different criteria by which they proceed to register. Example, Arnold Doppelganger Swangarion is a freshman. He therefore uses his trusty catalog when deciding on what courses to pick. Using his friend, the catalog, he finds out what basic studies courses he should take, as well as the required courses for his major. Having made his decision, he then pretends he's Leonard Nimoy and goes in search of his advisor.

Otto Penquist is a different story. He is a Senior and his basic studies are all out of the way. "All I have is one more requirement and the rest are electives. Now here if an interesting course—BIO 499 07—PRIMORDAL FUNGUS. Nah! It starts at eight in the morning. Here's an upper division Directed Study course, but it is a three-hour one. Wait a minute ! My friend Dawn told me she was going to register for it. Three hours with her wouldn't be bad. Direct my study towards her. Heh! Heh! Here's another good one—POL 472 01—WHAT'S THE IDEA, and that starts at 11:00. Let's see what else there is. FRICTION AS FILM, ETHNICS, both start in the afternoon. Ah! What a life!"

As we can see, all Otto cares about is allotting time for sleep, choosing courses with interesting names and courses that have students like Dawn in it.

"Well, it's my last semester," says Otto, "I should have some fun!"

What Otto fails to realize is that education is a valuable tool, not a toy to play with and then discard. To waste an education is not only to waste your tuition, but to waste the time of others and valuable years of your life. Thus, when you waste education like Otto, you're not prepared for the "real world," so to speak. No one will hire you if your brain is scattered like a dandelion blown in the wind.

Rather, employers prefer a trained and structured brain designed and catered to solve the most complex problems of a chosen field. This comes from a good solid education. But is Otto worried?

"Nah! I'm going to inherit my father's business."

Of course, some people are just born lucky.

On December 15th, I left my home, never to return-until January 9, 1983. Excuse: Winter Vacation; Reason: working for N.A.S.A. as an undercover National Security Protector or "Spy" in laymen's jargon. I was sent to upstate New York, close to Canada, and received the code name "Dr. Milos Greeley." Working with me, but in Key West, was Otto Penquist, who went by the code name of "Monica Petroleum." To secure the secrecy of our mission, we could only keep in contact via telepathy. Each of us received orders from L. Anagram Sardrich, who kept base in Fairfax, Virginia. Little did we know that John Gerard, who I met once before at a gynecological recreation center, was hot on our trail.

The mission was simple: to examine the moon from critical points on earth and to tabulate our results. Why the secrecy? A theory was circulating around N.A.S.A. and had to be checked out. It proposed that the moon has a strong gravitational pull on the Earth's ocean tides; it does not have a strong enough gravity to hold on to an atmosphere. Could the moon be an alien spaceship? Were the returning astronauts of the Apollo missions really extraterrestrials? After all, we do have pictures of Neil Armstrong climbing down the ladder of the lunar module and taking his first step on the moon, but who was taking the pictures? What of Richard M. Nixon? Did he not talk to the Apollo XI astronauts in a nationally televised phone conversation? Hos did he know the number? As there are no telephone lines from earth to the moon, how did the call get through? Was Nixon as alien being? Some political scholars theorize that the Watergate episode was caused by Nixon being replaced by a double, who, not knowing who he could trust, tried everything to stay in power.

One day, during the winter break, a lunar eclipse occurred around 5 a.m. E.S.T. Under close observation, one would observe the "moon" docking with a mother ship. I was about to report my findings when I heard a voice say, "So, Dr. Greeley, we meet again!" It was John Gerard, and his assistant Anonymous Rex enemies of the Rhineland Democracy.

"Gerard you fiend! What can you possibly hope to gain, siding with the aliens?" I asked him.

"Pathetic human! To be dominated by us will not be as bad for humans as it is to be dominated by others of your own species."

I asked, "When will all this take place?"

"On your birthday!" he responded. There was only one way out. I lifted my arms and they passed out, B.O. works.

As I telepathically communicated the situation to Otto, he took action. Again, under the guise of Monica Petroleum, he managed to set up several nuclear ballistic missiles aimed at the "moon." Getting together with L. Anagram Sardrich and C. Anagram Husyganes (no relation), a N.A.S.A. intelligence expert, and somewhat attractive female, Otto and I came up with a plan.

Destroy the Moon! However, we need your help, which is why I have revealed the mission. Send whatever cash you have (single girls just send pictures) to Destroy the Moon, Limited!

THE REAL LORD'S PRAYER

What the deuce?!? The "Original Aramaic Lord's Prayer." that can be found online at various websites is not original, not Aramaic, not a translation, and not the Lord's Prayer!

That's right, boys and girls! Things like this just piss me off! What can be found online at several sites (and off line in several books) stems for the most part from books by Neil Douglas-Klotz.

The transliteration is poor!

Anyone reading the English letters will not get a sense of what the words sound like

The translation is based on the Syriac version of the Lord's Prayer.

Syriac is a dialect of Aramaic, but it differs in some respects from Galilean and other Palestinian dialects of Aramaic, and so even to the extent that the Syriac prayer is Aramaic, it is not the original Aramaic.

If you want to really grasp the Lord's Prayer as Jesus uttered it in his own language, there is only one way to get even close to doing that: learn the ancient Palestinian dialect of Aramaic. Translating words from one language into another always involves some transformation of meaning. Also, you can't take the English version and translate it into 1stcentury Palestinian Greek, because the English version is itself a translation of New Testament Greek. You have to translate the New Testament Greek into 1st century Palestinian Aramaic, and then translate that into English. On top of that, the prayer found in Luke is slightly different than the one found in Matthew (which is more close to the original). You have to know what the New Testament Greek meant for the people of that time before translating it into 1st century Palestinian Greek. Many sites on line have this:

Abwun
"Oh Father, from whom the breath of life comes."

As poetic as that sounds, it is putting into the NT Greek a concept that is not there. Abwun simply means "Our Father," and comes from Abba, which means Daddy. Nothing more than that. Just Daddy. "Daddy" itself is a revolutionary concept for it's time. The Jewish people of that time (and even today) refer to the Almighty as G-d, or HaShem ("The Name"). To be on such intimate terms with God would be considered sacrilegious. Still, the word means "Our Daddy", not the nonsensical, "O Birther! Father-Mother of the Cosmos!" Really! No 1st century Palestinian rabbi would utter such twaddle, and, even if one did, no one would have bothered to follow him, let alone write down his prayer.

So, using the New Testament Greek Matthew's Gospel, I think I can safely say the Lord's Prayer probably was:

Abun d'bashmayo

Our Daddy, Who reigns over Heaven
Nethkadash ishmoch (or: Nethkadsah shamak. It's tricky)

Blessed is Your NameTithe malkuthog

May Your Kingdom come
Nehwe sebjonog

Your Will being done
Aykano d'bashmayo

on Earth just as it is in Heaven
Of bar'o Hab lan laghmo d'sunkonan yawmono

Allow us the bread we need today
yawmono Washboek lan ghauwbayn

Forgive our debts (Yes. It says, "debts," not "sins." of course, tradition says Matthew was a tax collector).
Waghtohain Aykano dof ghnan

because we forgive debtors
Shbakan lghayobain Oelo ta'el lan lnesjoeno

Prevent us from temptations
Elo fason lan men biesho

deliever us from the Evil One
Metul diloch ie malkoetho Oe ghaylo teshbughto Hoel 'olam 'olmien

Your kingdom. Your glory. Your power. Your song. For eternity.

That's the best I could do, and it wasn't easy, but some times the things I find on the internet just piss me off!

THE GOVERNMENT SHUTDOWN

The government shut down
Still I cannot find my mind. Some did laugh.
Some did frown
By shapes my words are known, I try.

The government shut down
but it was not scary
The souls of men go tumbling down, fumbling down
Alas, they are necessary.

The government shut down
Like birds with arms it seemed surrealistic
The more I've thought of him, the founder I've grown
good citizens do not go ballistic.

The government shut down
peach butter with cinnamon glistened in the sun
the fabled garb of Occidental renown
even if your nose starts to run.

The government shut down
But the baying was many miles away,
Goat entrails are brown
Nothing changed today.

CRYING OUT TO GOD

Your hope in my heart is the rarest treasure
Your Name on my tongue is the sweetest word
My choicest hours
Are the hours I spend with You.
Oh, my dearest Father, I can't live in this world
Without remembering You.
How can I endure the next world
Without seeing Your face?
I am a stranger in Your country
And lonely among Your worshippers.
The rituals are empty.
The prayers are too formulaic.
All I need is You.

LOVE

There is no more wonderful state of mind than Love. Love itself, being in love, feeling loved and lovely, all work together to create the highest and most happified state of existence. It is love that in one great sweep of the heartstrings brings into harmony the symphony of life, orchestrating and arranging all of life's disparate parts into one grand concord. In love, where the operative word is in, like being in New York or being in a play. True love is a place the lovers occupy, happy citizens of an extraordinary city. Love all around.

But then again, what do I know? I stll think that rain is wet.

A PRE-CHRISTMAS SPECIAL.
THE ADVENT ADVENTURE.

It was Advent, and this meant that it was time to prepare for the upcoming event of Christmas. Christmas is when Christians commemorate Jesus coming into the world (theologically speaking, He always was in the world, but this commemorates the event of the Incarnation, i.e., Jesus being born as a baby, a human. The union of divinity with humanity in Jesus), and Christmas is also a time when Christians prepare for the return of Jesus at the Second Coming, (Theologically speaking, Jesus never left the world, but the Second Coming is Jesus manifesting Himself in the physical sense). Christmas then is a time of good will and peace to all men, and even some women, but not all. Advent is the period beginning four Sundays before Christmas and observed by some Christians as a season of prayer and fasting. It is a time of preparation. The King is coming and all must be ready. For younger Christians that adults call children, Advent is the countdown to Christmas, and that means Santa Claus-the fat man from the north pole who breaks into houses, rips people off of cookies and milk, but always leaves toys and candy for the children. However, if your naughty in his sight, then you'll end up with coal in your stockings, but if your non-Christian, you'll end up with nothing. It was Advent, and all was not well.

"It's Advent," said Doctor Livingston, "and that means soon Santa Claus will be arriving. I hate Santa Claus, he keeps taking my milk and cookies but all I ever get is coal. Why? Because I'm a smoker. Santa says that good boys and girls should never smoke. Well I don't care about that, as I have a plan that will end Santa's activities!"

Doctor Livingston was a friend of the people who work in the Soviet Embassy. Through contacts at the embassy, Doctor Livingston became aware of a certain Soviet Espionage Agent called Rudolph the Red. Using the contacts at the embassy, Doctor Livingston made arrangements to meet Ruldolph the Red at a certain out of the way spot.

"What I want you to do," explained Livingston, "is to disguise yourself as a reindeer and lead Santa's sleigh into Soviet air space. As soon as the Soviets become aware that their air space has been violated, they will shoot the sleigh down."

"How will they know when we have entered if Santa flys his sleigh to low for the radar to pick up?"

"Wear this invention of mine," said Doctor Livingston. "It's guaranteed fool proof."

"It looks like a red nose."

"It is a red nose. Once activated, it will set off the radar system of the Soviet Union."

"That's pure genius Doc," said Rudolph.

"What kind of doctor are you anyway?"

"I'm a proctologist."

"What do I get for doing this job?" asked Rudolph.

"American jeans," was the reply.

"American jeans? I'll do it!"

Using a mariner's compass, Rudolph went to the north in hopes of getting to Santa's before his test flights. Once he arrived, he immediately disguised himself as a reindeer, and was able to join Santa's sleigh team. Rudolph was examining his nose when it accidentally went off. Santa noticed and approached him. "My number's up," thought Rudolph, but that was not the case.

"Rudolph with your nose so bright, won't you guide my sleigh tonight?" asked Santa.

Rudolph agreed and that night led thesleigh on it's test flight. Ralph the Elf couldn't help but wonder about Rudolph's nose. He was in charge of the electronic entertainment department and thought he had seen something familiar in one of his manuals. He looked through them all and saw an advertisement that read, "Fool Your Friends! Have them shot down by Soviets!" The item advertised looked amazingly like Rudolph's nose. Then a phone call came. Santa and his reindeer had been shot down and are being held captive by the Soviets. Ralph the Elf had no choice. He went into the violent toy section of the Elf workshop and came across the Sirch-Killer from the Future Doll. Building it to life size, Ralph took the emergency sleigh and led an army of elves and Sirch into the Soviet Union.

Meanwhile, news of Santa's captivity had reached the media, and they in their usual way broadcasted it across the world. Will there be a Christmas? was all the media kept askin, forgetting the fact that Christmas really had nothing to do with Santa Claus but with a Baby born in a manger almost 2000 years ago. Doctor Livingston was well pleased. "Now we'll see what happens," said the Doctor.

December 25, came and there were no presents under the tree, nor was there coal in the stockings. "I won!" exclaimed the Doctor with joy. The Doctor turned on the news only to discover Christmas Masses still being held and people on the streets still wishing each other good will. "How can this be?" pondered the Doctor. Unable to take anymore, Doctor

Livingston went out for a walk. Hearing voices from on top of the house, the confused proctologist looked up and on the roof saw Santa, Ralph, Sirch, a bunch of elves, and a tied up Rudolph. "Ho! Ho! Ho!" said Santa as two tons of coal were dropped on top of the Doctor. "Merry Christmas!" were Santa's last words as everyone but Rudolph took off.

Rudolph got loose and managed to dig out Doctor Livingston from the coal. "Sorry," said Rudolph, "but not even the Soviet Union can match the strength of angry elves and a doll named Sirch."

"Is that all you have to say?" yelled the Doctor.

"No," said Rudolph as he handed the Doctor a carton of cancerous cigarettes. "Merry Christmas."

Doctor Livingston thought for a moment and then said, "Merry Christmas."

THE APOCALYPSE
(OF THIS BOOK)

Genesis of Doom

It all began several years ago when the demented Otto Lawrence Penquist took pen and paper in hand and wrote to the Church of Gospel Ministry. He had previously seen their add in a gossip rag which stated that anyone could get free reverend credentials, and he decided to write for his.

"Soon," thought Otto, "I'll be a legal preacher. I will go among the masses spreading my message, and I'll be tax exempt as well."

It was not long before the Message of Penquist caught on, and he gained many followers. His message was that everyone has the capability of being God, and, in a sense, everyone is God. However, in order to tap into the God-element, a small donation was needed to Penquist's church. The fact that one is God and could become God was a real ego trip for some people and many donations were received. And the Message spread. Otto made his big mistake while taking a verse writing class. Having penned a poem entitled "Executed by Frogs," he revealed what a vile, corrupt person he really was. The, the instructor of the course and a man who managed to elude the yearbook the past couple of years, realized that the author of the poem and the preacher of the Message were one in the same. Having discussed the situation with an associate, they came up with a plan so elaborate and so complicated, that it was impossible for both of them to implement it. Forced to go for outside help, they found sympathetic ears with a group who called themselves Professors of English. This group after reading "Executed By Frogs," vowed to stop Penquist at all cost! As if an omen of good luck, the sunset started to work overtime until it collapsed.

The Assassin

"God, as generally conceived, cannot enjoy humor because He has perfect information. He can neither think nor have a sense of humor. The theological definition of God as perfect knowledge means He cannot proceed from one arrangement of information to a better one (that is thinking), nor can He be surprised (that is humor). It would be an insult to say that God could think!" That was the message Otto Lawrence Penquist preached to his followers on that day which would be his last.

Unknown to Penquist, the group that call themselves Professors of English had decided to eliminate him. This was due to them reading one of his poems entitled "Executed by Frogs," which showed what a vile and corrupt person he is. Searching through their records, they found a student that they thought could help them in their plans. He was known as the Assassin and also as the Rock. Hailing from Connecticut, he had returned there due to the fact that some higher up panjandrums were throwing primordial fungus in his face. Dr. Buster Brown went up to Connecticut to convince the Assassin to come back to Saint Leo. He did by impressing him with an incredible display of hockey. The next step was to get equipment for the Assassin

"I used to play hockey for the Army," said Dr. Brown. "I should have some connections there." And so he did. At a small army base in Upstate New York, the Purchasing Agents received a notice that they were to order up a thermal nuclear device, disguised as a ceramic mold for a bear, and ship \ it to Dr. Brown at Saint Otto. This would have gone right through if the Procurement Office weren't using Army issued typewriters. The typewriters were constantly on the brink, this corresponded with the bad vibes the one whose code name was Code Name would get. Then when the typewriters were fixed, they would break down as soon as the summer help would get hold of it. Finally it arrived.

The plan was for the Assassin, now enrolled as a student again, to pretend that he was one of Penquist' followers. He would then give the bear as a gift to Penquist. All would have gone well, except for one thing; the Assassin, unable to get cigarettes to support his habit, suffered a nicotine fit. He was unable to pull off the job.

This fact did not go unnoticed by the Professors of English. They decided to break out the M-16s and would have if the M-16s weren't removed during the Quang Rebellion of 1974. It was suggested that a balloon be sent up carrying aerosol cans which would end up destroying the ozone in the atmosphere, and Penquist would end up fried—but so would the innocent.

It was then that they came up with The Plan plan.

"Assuming there is a God, wouldn't He be rather offended by someone who says that He has no sense of Humor, and that He can't think? I suggest we tell him," pronounced the late Dr. M.S.

"How do we do that?" asked Dr. Howovitz Zed.

"By praying," responded the still late M.S.

"Are you off your nut? We represent the most intellectual minds on campus, let alone the universe. We could read Omni magazine and understand it, were it still in print. If we're caught praying, what would become of the word Stoic?" said some Unknown teacher (although it was really a student in disguise).

"Ah! But we don't have to pray. It is Lent. Surely someone has told Him by now," said a professor who was disguised as another professor.

"I hope so," said Jim Porto who was disguised as the first student.

Someone did manage to tell God about Otto in their prayers. God became furious. "Get that Penquist over here!" He shouted.

"But Huge One," said an angel disguised as Professor Tyson Anderson, "Only the dead are allowed down here."

"I know that," said God, disguised as a cloud.

And so it was that Otto Lawrence Penquist died. It seems God did have a sense of humor after all.

The Phoenix

The Reverend Otto Lawrence Penquist had, died, and the news quickly spread around the campus. He had died, or so the story went, by slipping on a banana peel. Some said that the banana peel was put there by the Hand of God, just to prove that He had a sense of humor. Many of the followers of Otto claimed that he slipped for our sins. Many of the other followers of Otto claimed that the followers who wanted to make Otto a martyr were, "out of their heads". Then there were the followers of Otto who managed to preserve the banana peel and use it as a sacred relic. Although Otto never made any connection with Divinity (he was only interested with making connection with the checkbooks of his followers), some of his followers wanted to make him out to be a super prophet. One of Otto's followers was Eduardo E. Edwards and he knew he had to act fast.

Eduardo E. Edwards was an R.A.—Resurrection Assistant—and was in charge of the temple prostitutes. Although Otto never had a temple, he claimed to have the blueprints for one, but before he laid down the cornerstone, he wanted to break the temple prostitutes in. He assigned Edwards to be in charge of the temple prostitutes. Why Otto chose Edwards is at this time unknown, but it is reported that Duffy said that he had "a good feeling" about the whole thing. In any case, Duffy was excellent at his job, and even received a raise. When the reports reached him about the death of Otto, he was naturally upset, but when the reports came to him about the followers of Otto who wanted to make him a super prophet, he became outraged. He knew that Otto was just like him in every way, except that Otto liked to sleep in closets. There had to bee something he could do to correct the situation, and there was.

Eduardo E. Edwards was a friend of Dr. Whologan. Dr. Whogan was a Lord of Time from another planet which was known for its rather liberal stance in politics, and he traveled around in a T.A.R.D.I.S. (Time and Relative Dimension In Space) which was shaped like a locker that one can find in small private airports in St. Louis. Dr. Whologan was using the cover of a Professor of History, but let Edwards know who he really was. Edwards didn't believe him at first, until he sat in the TARDIS. The TARDIS was capable of going anywhere in time and to any planet. Duffy told Dr. Whologan that if they could go back in time to before the banana peel incident, then everything would be on the right track. They both went into the TARDIS, and Dr. Whogan set the controls. When they opened the door, they found themselves in a temple in ancient Israel, circa 970 B.C.

"Must have slipped somewhere," explained the Dr. "But that's alright. The high priest is coming and is about to say the name of God. He only does it about once a year, and no one is supposed to hear him, so they remain outside. So sacred is the name of God. Good thing I brought along a universal language translator. SHH! Here he comes."

The high priest entered the inner sanctuary and said the name of God. Cor Bett.

"Cor Bett!" exclaimed Duffy, "That doesn't even sound Jewish!" Dr. Whogan approached the high priest, so startled was the priest that he thought that the Dr. was an angel.

"Listen," said Dr. Whogan, "God's name is Yahweh."

"Why, 'Yahweh'?" asked the priest.

"Because God's name is so secret, we're going to call it something else so no one else finds out."

"I get it," said the priest, who didn't get it really. With that, the Dr. and his companion left.

Meanwhile, God was down in Heaven trying to impress the soul of Penquist with some jokes, just to prove He had a sense of humor. Unfortunately, God was a bad comedian.

"Listen, I know your trying your best and all that, but it's getting to be a real drag trying to spend eternity with You cracking these jokes of Yours," said Otto.

"All right," said God, "Tell you what I'll do. There is a friend of yours, Eduardo E. Edwards, he's been trying to correct the situation that caused your earthly demise. I sent him and his friend back to ancient Israel, but I'll let him succeed under certain conditions. First, you can't be corrupt, second, any money you make goes to some good causes, and third, you tell everyone I have a great sense of humor."

"Oh, come on now—" said Otto's soul.

"Alright. Hear the one about—"

"O.K., I'll tell them, but it's not logical, you know."

"Good. Now your going to have to get rid of the temple prostitutes."

"No sweat. Edwards is probably tired by now."

"Good. Off you go then," said God.

The TARDIS arrived on the scene of the banana peel as Otto was approaching. Edwards removed the banana peel and Otto never slipped.

"Ah, Eduardo," said Otto, "Just the person I was looking for. I decided to reform. We're going to have to let the temple prostitutes go."

"That's alright," said Edwards. "I was getting tired anyway."

So it was that Otto never died, thanks to Dr. Whogan and the unseen Hand of God, and, of course, the man called Eduardo E. Edwards.

SOME TIME IN THE PRESENT—MAYBE A DAY OR TWO AGO

There I was in my study, and I came across my box of mad memories. I removed my old mood ring and amazing battery operated hypno ring (which constantly changes bright colors). They still fit! Later, I went out to do shopping and was enjoying this spring like day. I had on one of my black caps. As I was approaching the door of a local eatery, I noticed a young couple and their even younger son approaching the door. The father was leading the way, but his back was to the door. I held the door open for them. My left hand held the door, while I stood there with my cap on, and my right hand was holding my cane. The look on his face made me think he thought i was funny, so I said, "Evening, Governor!" The boy, who looked around four, noticed my hypno ring and exclaimed to his mom, "What a cool guy!" Getting that reaction from a little child made me feel like I was in Heaven—and I probably was.

THOSE DARN CATS

It was six in the morning. I felt tremendous pressure in the center of my chest. Was this a heart attack? Has Death finally come? No. It was my fourteen pound cat, Pedro. I thought, "He's being unusually affectionate." Then he produced my wallet and car keys. Foolishly, I had taught him my PIN, but he is an indoor cat and has never seen an ATM, nor would he have knowledge on how to operate one. The cat can hardly drive as it is. Since it was early, I refused to go downstairs and feed him. It was obvious that he was trying to tell me he wanted me to buy him food. Three hours later, despite his constant threats, I went downstairs, only to discover that the cats have at least a week left in cat food. Pedro! Always thinking with his stomach. However, I noticed my human food will run out after breakfast tomorrow. Later in the afternoon, I went off to BJ's, because I always save a lot of money when I buy food there (Product Placement), and the food is great (Product placement), especially the cheese.

Pedro has developed a habit, which I find amusing. When he is finished or dissatisfied with his food, he would cover it with something—a napkin, a place mat, a horse head, whatever he can find nearby. When I came home from shopping, I realized I did not buy any cat food at all. As I was putting the food I purchased in the cabinets, refrigerator, freezer, etc., I noticed Pedro's bowl. On it was a page torn out of a book. It was from the Holy Quran! Did Pedro go into my personal library of sacred books, go to one of my three personally translated

Qurans, and personally rip out a page of the Quran? I'd take that personal, but then I noticed the page. It was from a Quran, but not from the text. It was from a forward, and it was not written in English or Arabic. It was written in Catonese, by a Professor Fluffers. In the corner of the room, there stood Pedro. He was standing on his hind legs, and holding the kitty litter trowel, and I could tell by his expression he was angry that I did not buy cat food. I quickly doodled a doodle of Mohammed about to do something nasty with a piece of bacon (I had him putting mustard on it and about to eat it). I said, "All right, Pedro, if that is your real name. I have here a depiction of Mohammed, and I am prepared to look at it!" Pedro hissed. I continued, "When I am done looking at it, I will then show it to you!!!' Pedro howled. If he were human, he probably would have screamed, "Noooooooooooooooooo!" Instead, he threw his turban across the room and stormed upstairs. My other cat just slept threw the whole thing, completely detached from what was going on, but she's a Buddhist, so she would be that way.

CPSIA information can be obtained at www.ICGtesting.com
Printed in the USA
BVOW07s0339250614

357309BV00001B/27/P